AMERICA'S GREATEST GAME

**The Real Story
of Football
and the NFL**

BY JAMES BUCKLEY, JR.
FOREWORD BY JERRY RICE

HYPERION BOOKS FOR CHILDREN
NEW YORK

Library of Congress Cataloging-in-Publication Data
Buckley, James Jr.
   America's greatest game: the real story of football and the National Football League/by James Buckley, Jr. — 1st ed.
   p. cm.
   Summary: A historical overview of how the game of football has evolved through the years and how the National Football League began.
   ISBN 0-7668-0433-5
   1. National Football League—History—Juvenile literature. 2. Football—United States—History—Juvenile literature. [1. National Football League—History. 2. Football—History.]
   I. Title.
GV955.5.N35B83   1998
796.332`64`0973—dc21   97-47744 CIP

Printed in Hong Kong.

First Edition
1 3 5 7 9 10 8 6 4 2

Produced by the Publishing Group of NFL Properties, Inc., Los Angeles, California: Vice President: John Wiebusch; General Manager: Bill Barron; Managing Editor: Chuck Garrity, Sr.; Project Editor/Writer: James Buckley, Jr; Executive Art Director: Brad Jansen; Associate Art Director: Evelyn Javier; Director-Manufacturing: Dick Falk; Director-Print Services: Tina Dahl.

The National Football League, the NFL Shield logo, "NFL," "NFC," "AFC," and "Super Bowl" are trademarks of the National Football League. The NFL team names, logos, helmets, and uniform designs are trademarks of the teams indicated.

Photographs: T. Alexander, 23; Thomas Allen, 14; Eric Lars Bakke, 8; John Biever, 3; Vernon J. Biever, 52; George Brace, 12; Peter Brouillet, 40, 58, 61, 63; College Football Hall of Fame, 16; Greg Crisp, 25; Tom Croke, 41; Bill Cummings, 23; Scott Cunningham, 23; David Drapkin, 7, 9; E.B. Graphics, 46; Malcolm Emmons, 22; Bob Ewell, 24; Craig Fears, 53; James Flores, 21; Tracy Frankel, 4, 52; Gerald Gallegos, 9; George Gojkovich, 4, 22; David Martin Graham, 33; Richard Graulich/Palm Beach Post, 45; Jon Hayt, 5, 42; Thearon Henderson, 38; Paul Jasienski, 27; Allen Kee, 35, 37; Al Kooistra, 40; Ross Lewis, 14; George Long, 1; Al Messerschmidt, 5–6, 9, 25, 33, 35, 53, 57, 60; Peter Read Miller, 34; Tom Miller, 33; Steven Murphy, 25, 49; NFL Photos, 10–14, 17–19; Daryl Norenberg, 17, 20; Joe Patronite, 7, 50–51; Hy Peskin/Sports Illustrated, 14; Pro Football Hall of Fame, 11, 30; Mitchell Reibel, 24; John H. Reid III, 41; Bob Rosato, 48, 56, 59, 62; Todd Rosenberg, 23–25, 36, 39; Manny Rubio, 7; Aggie Skirball, 9; Paul Spinelli/NFLP, 37, 44, 53, 63; Brian Spurlock, 55; R.H. Stagg, 22; Allen Dean Steele, 38; David Stluka, 36, 49, 54; Al Tielmans, 9, 32, 52; Tony Tomsic, 15, 18-19, 47; Greg Trott, 39, 55; Ron Vesely, 63; Ben Waddle, 54; Gaylon Wampler, 7; Scott D. Weaver, 43; Yale Athletic Association, 16; Michael Zagaris, 22, 49, 58, 59.
Illustrations: page 15: Johnee Bee; page 21: Merv Corning; pages 28–29: Jon Watson.
Cover Illustration: Roger Huyssen and Gerard Huerta/2H Studio.

Contents

▶ On a cold day at Soldier Field, Chris Zorich's sweaty head appears to be on fire; it actually is escaping body heat.

The Game I Love

I love running, lifting weights, practicing, and watching game films.

I love playing football, running downfield, catching passes, scoring touchdowns, and winning! I love playing this wonderful game.

Don't get me wrong. I appreciate the records I've set, and I enjoy sharing Super Bowls with my family and my teammates. The honors I've received as a result of my efforts are very gratifying.

But that takes a backseat to the game.

People ask me why I work so hard in the offseason, why I run up and down hills and go to the gym every day, when I could be playing golf or taking vacations.

I do all that because I love the game. I love breaking from the huddle, standing at my position, waiting for the snap, and beating the cornerback. I can't wait for the play to begin and to run my route. I can feel the urgency to score.

Then the ball is in the air. I can see the seams of the ball, and the laces spinning. I'm concentrating so hard it's as if I'm in slow motion. Total tranquility. My hands go up to catch the ball, and at that moment, I'm as happy as I can be. I'm playing the game I love.

Jerry Rice

CHAPTER ONE

Play Football!

An All-American Game for Everyone

It is getting dark and there is time for just one more play.

"C'mon," your friends say, "call the play. We gotta get home!"

"All right, all right, just a sec," you say.

You look past your huddle and see the other team lining up to stop you. If you score, you win the game and dinner will taste much better.

You've been out here since the minute school ended. Just you, your friends, and a football. By now, the knees of your jeans are caked with mud. There is enough dirt under your nails to grow vegetables. And you're loving every minute of it.

▲ Football players don't let a little thing like rain stand in the way of a good game.

"What's the matter, you chicken?" the biggest player on the other team yells. "Let's go!"

That does it. You look at your teammates. They all stare at you, waiting. Why? Because you're the quarterback. You're the man.

You're Dan Marino. You're John Elway or Steve Young or Kordell Stewart. You're the star at Michigan, at Nebraska, at Florida State. You're the local high school hero. You've watched all of them do it, and you know that you can, too.

The sun is dipping behind the trees at the end of the park. The wind is picking up a little as evening comes. You imagine thousands of screaming fans, just like at every football game, are pleading with you to score.

You look around the huddle once more. "Okay, you guys, on three," you say.

"Everybody go long!"

▲ Kids of all sizes play football in leagues across America.

▲ John Elway handing off to Terrell Davis? No, just some Florida peewee players. More than 4 million boys and girls play youth-league football in America.

▲ Girls can't play football? Think again. Watch this young lady run by a defender.

◀ "Good game, good game, good game, good game..." A postgame handshake between two North Carolina teams.

Who needs pads? Flag football can be just as much fun as tackle.

What is the best part of football? Why, playing on a team, of course.

▲ When your mom is calling, it's getting dark, and your team is trailing by just a few points, there is only one play for your team to call: Everybody go long!

▲ Make sure you throw the football and not a snowball.
▼ Hope he's not playing against a team called the Sharks.

WHEN I WAS A KID

NFL players remember what it was like before they were pros.

Mark Brunell, Jaguars

Mark's scrambling and passing abilities make him one of the NFL's top quarterbacks. He grew up in Santa Maria, California. "I'll never forget the first time I played quarterback. I was so nervous because it was a new position for me. I was shaking the first time I took a snap. But it turned out all right, we won a few games, and I had a lot of fun. That's when I knew I wanted to keep playing quarterback."

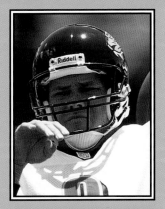

Herman Moore, Lions

Herman, a four-time Pro Bowl wide receiver, set an NFL record in 1995 with 123 receptions. He grew up in Danville, Virginia. "Believe it or not, I started on my high school team as a kicker. I also high-jumped for our track team. That really helped when I became a receiver. I found I could outjump other players."

Derrick Thomas, Chiefs

Derrick, a nine-time Pro Bowl linebacker, set an NFL record in 1990 with 7 sacks in one game. He grew up in Miami, Florida. "I was in and out of trouble from the time I was 10 until I was in high school. And I really loved sports. Then getting in trouble took football and sports away from me. I had to make a decision on what I was going to do. Missing football made me realize what I had been doing wrong. I made the choice to go from there and really be somebody. Football was my way out."

CHAPTER TWO

Football's Early Years

From Hupmobiles to Super Bowls

▲ Harold (Red) Grange, the "Galloping Ghost," was the first college superstar to become an NFL superstar, too.

Who Invented Football?

Football today is a colorful, action-packed game with rules that help make it safe and fair.

That was not always true, however.

Football's roots are in the games of rugby and soccer as played in England. The first recognized college football game in America took place in 1869 when Princeton and Rutgers squared off. Each team had 25 players in a contest that was a mixture of soccer, rugby, and football. The game soon caught on at colleges throughout the eastern United States.

The games, however, often looked like giant free-for-alls. Everybody played by different rules, leading to chaos.

It was time to get organized.

In 1876, the first written rules for football were

▲ A typical football uniform from the 1890s.

adopted. A man named Walter Camp probably had more to do with "inventing" football than anyone. Camp was a star player at Yale University, and later a coach at Yale and other schools. He helped create the idea of "downs," and helped decide the point value of each score.

Even with the new rules, the game was ponderous, tough, and grueling. Players wore few pads, and everyone played both offense and defense.

In Camp's day, football was all about running. Almost every play ended up with a huge pile-up on the ball carrier. Passing the football did not become legal until 1906.

After passing became popular, however, the game of football speeded up and spread out. It became safer for players and more exciting for fans.

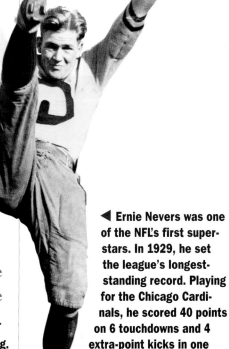

◀ Ernie Nevers was one of the NFL's first superstars. In 1929, he set the league's longest-standing record. Playing for the Chicago Cardinals, he scored 40 points on 6 touchdowns and 4 extra-point kicks in one game.

◀ Football or free-for-all? The first games of what would someday become football were a combination of rugby and wrestling.

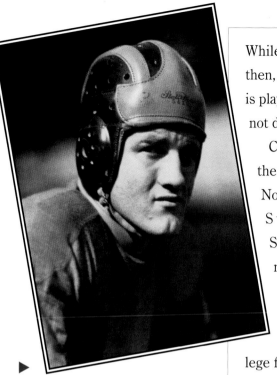

Bronko Nagurski. Was there ever a better name for a football player? Bronko was a star running back for the Bears and one of the first players inducted into the Pro Football Hall of Fame.

Among the NFL's early—and short-lived—teams were the Evansville Crimson Giants, the Oorang Indians, the Pottsville Maroons, the Louisville Brecks, and the Providence Steam Roller.

While there have been minor rule changes since then, football soon became much like the game that is played today. Of course, back then the players did not do touchdown dances.

College football was the most popular form of the game until after World War II. Schools such as Notre Dame, Yale, Minnesota, Michigan, Army, Stanford, and Southern California were national champions with fans from coast to coast. College football became a national passion for fans, even if they were not in school. For the players, it was a different matter.

The NFL Is Born

In 1920, a group of sportsmen who loved the game of football wanted to form a professional league. They met on September 17, 1920, in a store that sold cars called Hupmobiles.

From that meeting, the organization that became the NFL was born.

Most of the men who were there that day owned or played for semiprofessional football teams from

the Midwest. They called the new league the American Professional Football Association. In 1922, they changed the name to the National Football League. Olympic champion and football star Jim Thorpe was the league's first president.

Cities such as Akron, Dayton, and Muncie boasted teams with names like Pros, Triangles, and Fly-

▲ Before 1920, teams such as the Canton Bulldogs (above) were semipro clubs that played whenever they could arrange a game.

ers. The clubs that became today's Arizona Cardinals and Chicago Bears also were part of the NFL in 1920.

In the early days of the NFL, players wore leather helmets or no helmets at all. There were no facemasks and no artificial turf.

Stars in the early NFL all played more than one position. In the early days of football, almost all the players played both offense and defense. A running back also might be a cornerback; a center might be a defensive tackle, too. Most players were on the field for the entire game. It took great strength and stamina to play in the early NFL.

What else was different then? The teams traveled on trains and buses. Players often had to fix

"RED" GRANGE
CHICAGO BEARS
VS.
"BUCK" BAILEY
SAN FRANCISCO TIGERS

KEZAR STADIUM

Price 25¢

Official ... Team

OFFICIAL
NATIONAL FOOTBALL LEAGUE
ROSTER and RECORD MANUAL

1941

Clarke Hinkle
(Green Bay Packers)

▲ Red Grange always got top billing whenever he played.

▶ By the 1940s, the NFL had become a successful league, with an annual record book.

their own equipment or sew their own uniforms. Players and coaches had second jobs in the offseason—and often during the season, too. It was a difficult way to play, but the players did it because they loved the game.

No matter how different it was, it still was football: A team needed to go 10 yards to make a first down. The field was 100 yards from goal line to goal line. A touchdown was worth six points. Then as now, teams of great athletes tried to move the ball toward the goal line, while other teams tried to stop them.

The NFL Grows Up

The NFL grew slowly in the 1920s and 1930s. College football still was more popular, but the NFL was catching on with America's sports fans. Stars such as Red Grange, Jim Thorpe, Bronko Nagurski, Sid Luckman, and Ernie Nevers helped the league win new fans.

Grange especially helped the NFL become popular. After becoming the most famous college player in America, he joined the NFL. Huge crowds attended all of his games.

13

▲ Quarterback Sid Luckman (right) led the Chicago Bears to four NFL titles in the 1940s, including a 73–0 victory in the 1940 NFL Championship Game that set an NFL record for most points.

▲ The first footballs were rounder and heavier than today's models. As the ball became more pointed, passing it became more popular.

How the Helmet Has Changed

1920s

The first helmets were made of leather, with ear cups and not much padding. Not until 1940 did every NFL player wear a helmet.

1950s

Hard plastic helmets began to be used in the 1950s. A single metal or plastic facemask helped keep players out of the dentist's office. Beginning with the Rams in 1948, teams began to decorate their helmets.

1960s

Better padding inside and a bigger facemask were added to the helmet. Stronger plastics made it even safer and more comfortable.

1998

Today's helmets are custom-fitted for each player. Air-filled pockets mold around the players' heads. Larger, stronger facemasks often are combined with plastic visors.

▲ As Baltimore's Alan Ameche fell to the end zone to seal the Colts' overtime victory in the 1958 NFL Championship Game, NFL popularity began to boom.

Many NFL players stopped their playing careers to fight in World War II from 1941–45. More than 600 players joined the military. Many joined the fighting, while others were assigned to play on Armed Forces teams to entertain troops. Jack Lummus of the Giants, who was killed on Iwo Jima, was awarded the Congressional Medal of Honor.

After the war, the popularity of the NFL boomed. A rival league, the All-America Football Conference, started in 1946. The AAFC folded in 1950, and three AAFC teams joined the NFL: the Cleveland Browns, the San Francisco 49ers, and the Baltimore Colts.

A new invention called television helped more people enjoy football. The first NFL game was televised in 1939. The game between the Philadelphia Eagles and Brooklyn Dodgers could be seen only in about 1,000 homes in the New York City area. But it was a beginning. By the 1950s, television and football became a match made in heaven.

The 1958 NFL Championship Game between the Colts and Giants was televised nationwide. Millions of people were able to watch NFL action in their homes, joining the screaming thousands at New York's Yankee Stadium.

The game turned out to be a thrilling overtime battle, transforming football into a truly national sport. By the time Colts running back Alan Ameche scored the winning touchdown to give Baltimore 23–17 victory, the NFL was here to stay.

The Super 'Ball'?

In 1960, the American Football League was started. In January, 1967, the NFL and AFL champions played each other for the first time. (The two leagues became one in 1970.) The game needed a name that would make it stand out.

Kansas City Chiefs owner Lamar Hunt saw his daughter playing with a bouncy rubber toy called a "Super Ball." At a meeting a few days later, the subject of the AFL-NFL game came up. Hunt referred to the game as "Super Bowl" and the name stuck.

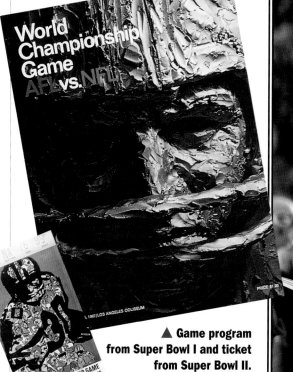

▲ Game program from Super Bowl I and ticket from Super Bowl II.
▶ Coach Vince Lombardi is carried off the field after Super Bowl II.

FOOTBALL'S EARLY HEROES

▲ **Glenn (Pop) Warner**
With 319 victories in 44 years, Pop Warner was one of the most successful college coaches of all time. The coach at several colleges from 1895–1938, he invented many football plays and strategies still used today. One of America's largest youth football programs is named in his honor.

▶ **Walter Camp**
Walter Camp is credited with leading the push for the use of "downs," planned plays, and the center snap, among other things. Camp coached the Yale University team from 1888–1891.

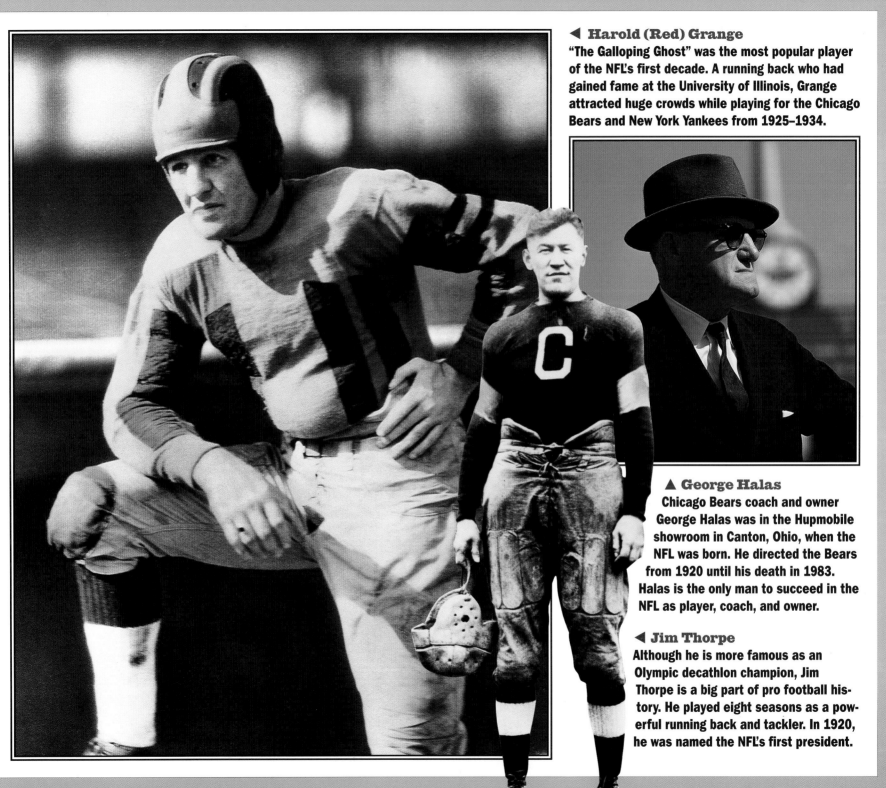

◄ Harold (Red) Grange

"The Galloping Ghost" was the most popular player of the NFL's first decade. A running back who had gained fame at the University of Illinois, Grange attracted huge crowds while playing for the Chicago Bears and New York Yankees from 1925–1934.

▲ George Halas

Chicago Bears coach and owner George Halas was in the Hupmobile showroom in Canton, Ohio, when the NFL was born. He directed the Bears from 1920 until his death in 1983. Halas is the only man to succeed in the NFL as player, coach, and owner.

◄ Jim Thorpe

Although he is more famous as an Olympic decathlon champion, Jim Thorpe is a big part of pro football history. He played eight seasons as a powerful running back and tackler. In 1920, he was named the NFL's first president.

FOOTBALL'S EARLY HEROES

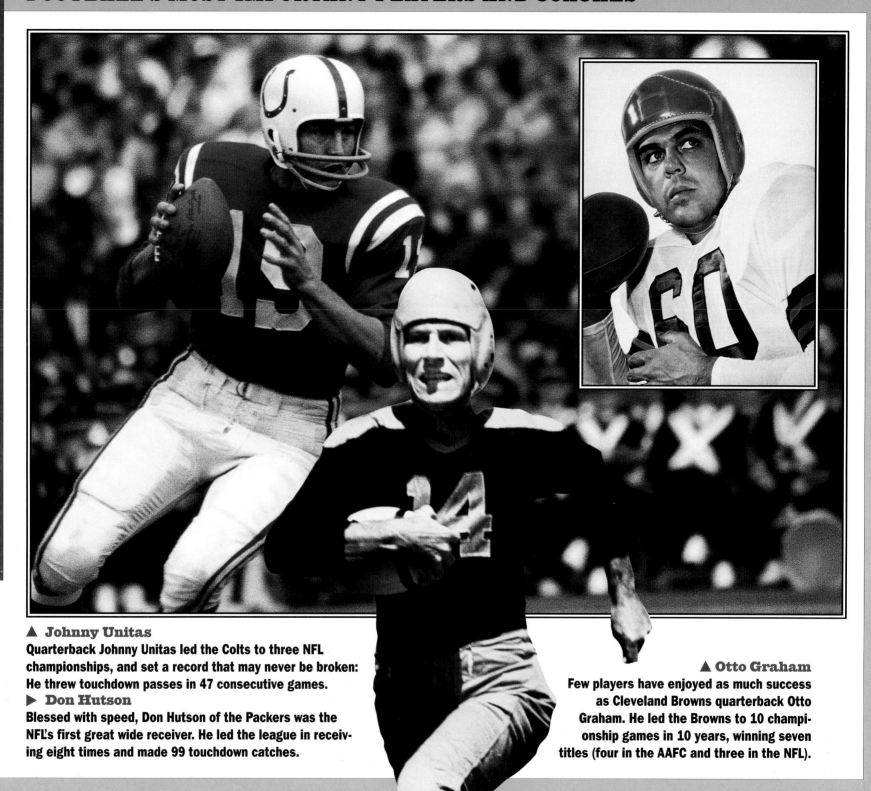

▲ **Johnny Unitas**
Quarterback Johnny Unitas led the Colts to three NFL championships, and set a record that may never be broken: He threw touchdown passes in 47 consecutive games.

▶ **Don Hutson**
Blessed with speed, Don Hutson of the Packers was the NFL's first great wide receiver. He led the league in receiving eight times and made 99 touchdown catches.

▲ **Otto Graham**
Few players have enjoyed as much success as Cleveland Browns quarterback Otto Graham. He led the Browns to 10 championship games in 10 years, winning seven titles (four in the AAFC and three in the NFL).

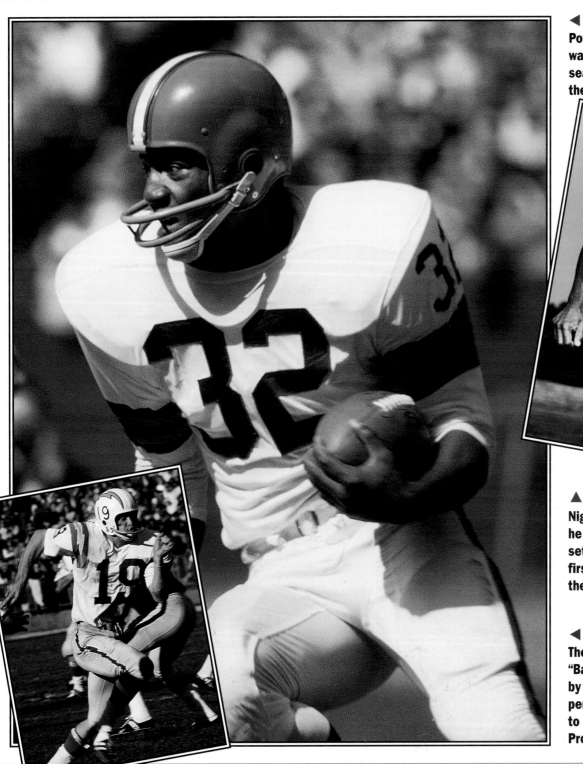

◄ Jim Brown

Powerful Cleveland Browns running back Jim Brown was the NFL rushing champion in eight of his nine seasons from 1957–1965. When he retired, he was the NFL's all-time leading rusher.

▲ Dick (Night Train) Lane

Night Train Lane had little football experience when he joined the Rams in 1952. But he learned quickly, setting an NFL record with 14 interceptions in his first season. The hard-hitting cornerback played in the NFL from 1952–1965.

◄ Lance Alworth (inset)

The San Diego Chargers' wide receiver known as "Bambi" was perhaps the greatest player produced by the AFL. Lance Alworth averaged nearly 19 yards per catch. He combined speed and leaping ability to become the first AFL player be inducted into the Pro Football Hall of Fame.

CHAPTER THREE

NFL's Modern Era

Pro Football Hits the Big Time

> "You've thought about it and you've dreamed about it. And then it happens. Nobody can beat you. You just can't wait for the final seconds to tick off."
>
> — Lance Alworth on winning a Super Bowl

In the 1950s, television helped make football more popular than ever. In the 1960s, the Super Bowl took the game to the stratosphere. The game began as a battle between the champions of two rival leagues. It soon became football's most important game and America's number-one unofficial national holiday. The history of the NFL's last four decades is the history of the Super Bowl.

The 1960s: Packer Power and Namath's 'I Guarantee It'

Led by legendary coach Vince Lombardi, the Green Bay Packers of the 1960s were one of the most dominant teams in NFL history. The team won five of

▲ Bart Starr was the MVP of Super Bowls I and II.

seven NFL titles from 1961–67. Their offense was led by quarterback Bart Starr, while linebacker Ray Nitschke anchored the defense. Seven other Hall of Fame players performed for Green Bay.

After the 1966 season, the Packers won Super Bowl I, defeating the Chiefs. They triumphed again the next year over the Raiders.

In Super Bowl III, the AFL's New York Jets were up against the NFL's Baltimore Colts. The Colts were supposed to win. But Jets quarterback Joe Namath had other ideas.

"We will win this game. I guarantee it," he said a few days before the game.

Most people thought he was crazy, but "Broadway Joe" proved them wrong. The Jets' stunning 16–7

◀ Joe Namath's white shoes, his rocket arm, and his "guarantee" of a Super Bowl III win helped make the Super Bowl super.

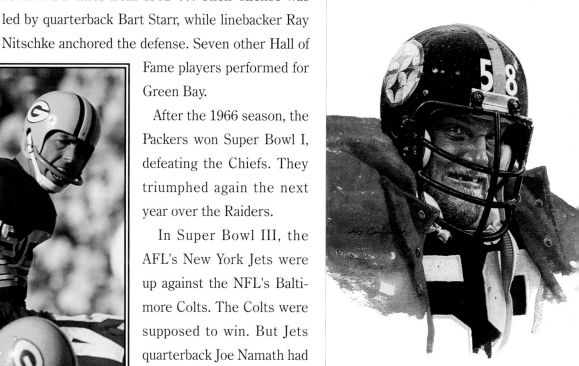

▲ The Steelers' grizzled Hall of Fame linebacker Jack Lambert was a symbol of the link between football's rugged past and its high-powered future.

▲ Coach Don Shula led the Dolphins to the NFL's only perfect season in 1972.

▶ The 1980s belonged to Joe Montana, one of the most popular and successful NFL players ever. He led the 49ers to four Super Bowl championships.

upset gave the AFL a big boost in respect, and made sports fans take even more notice of the big game.

The 1970s: Perfection and Steel

Beginning with the 1970 season, the merger of the NFL and the AFL became official. The NFL was made up of two conferences, the AFC and the NFC.

In 1972, the Miami Dolphins put together the only undefeated, untied season in NFL history. They wrapped up a perfect 17–0 record with a 14–7 victory over Washington in Super Bowl VII. The Dolphins were led by coach Don Shula (who retired in 1995 as the

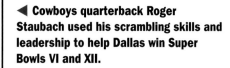
◀ Cowboys quarterback Roger Staubach used his scrambling skills and leadership to help Dallas win Super Bowls VI and XII.

▲ Running back Franco Harris was the bedrock of a Steelers' running game that helped win four Super Bowls in six seasons. He is seventh all-time in the NFL in rushing.

▲ Seahawks wide receiver Steve Largent set many of the records that Jerry Rice later broke. He wasn't the biggest receiver, but he was one of the most dependable.

NFL's all-time winningest coach, with 347 victories).

The rest of the 1970s were dominated by the Pittsburgh Steelers. They won four Super Bowls in six years, using a long-bomb offense led by quarterback Terry Bradshaw and a powerful running game keyed by Franco Harris. Pittsburgh's "Steel Curtain" defense, led by tackle Mean Joe Greene and linebacker Jack Lambert, was one of the best defenses in NFL history. Seven players from those Steelers teams, plus former coach Chuck Noll, are in the Pro Football Hall of Fame.

In 1976, two new teams, the Seattle Seahawks and Tampa Bay Buccaneers, joined the NFL, bringing the number of teams to 28.

The Super Bowl and television, the two forces that had built the NFL into an international success, continued to come together. Super Bowl XII in January, 1978, was watched by more people than any other show in television history to that time.

▲ Super Bowl XXII MVP Doug Williams of the Redskins.

▲ Big William (Refrigerator) Perry in Super Bowl XX.

▲ Phil Simms set passing records in Super Bowl XXI.

The 1980s: Joe and Jerry

In the 1980s, the San Francisco 49ers, led by quarterback Joe Montana, won four Super Bowls. Montana engineered a last-minute comeback to win Super Bowl XXIII. He also guided the team to a record 55 points in its Super Bowl XXIV victory over Denver. Montana often teamed with Jerry Rice, the NFL's career receiving leader.

The Washington Redskins won two Super Bowls in the decade. In Super Bowl XXII, the Redskins put on one of the most impressive offensive displays in league history. In the second quarter, quarterback Doug Williams threw 4 touchdown passes, while running back Timmy Smith added a 58-yard touch-

"Football is a great life. It's much easier than working for a living. Just think— they pay you good money to eat well, stay in shape, and have fun."

— Hugh McElhenny
Hall of Fame running back
1952-1964

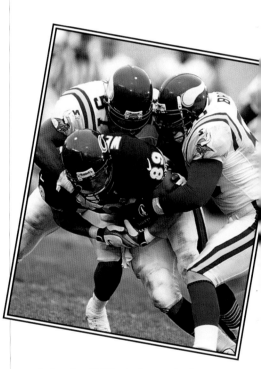

▲ A pair of Vikings demonstrate a tackle on a Chicago Bears pass receiver.

A strong arm and a will of iron have made Brett Favre a two-time NFL most valuable player. The Packers' quarterback led his team to victory in Super Bowl XXXI, and in 1997 he became the first quarterback to record four consecutive seasons with 30 or more touchdown passes.

▲ Minnesota wide receiver Cris Carter set an NFL record (later broken by Herman Moore) with 122 catches in 1994. He is fifth all time in touchdown catches.

▲ In only three seasons, Denver running back Terrell Davis has become one of the NFL's best players. The two-time Pro Bowl player has had three 1,000-yard seasons, and won the AFC rushing title in 1996 and 1997.

down run. The Redskins scored 35 points in 15 minutes.

Another newsmaking team in the decade was the 1985 Chicago Bears. The fun-loving personality of the Bears didn't hide the fact that they had a powerful defense and a strong offense. In defeating New England 46-10 in Super Bowl XX, the Bears allowed the Patriots only 7 rushing yards.

Although his team never played in a Super Bowl, Seattle wide receiver Steve Largent was one of the best players of the 1970s and 1980s. When he retired, he was the NFL's all-time leader in receptions, receiving yardage, and touchdown catches.

The 1990s: Cowboys Ride Again

The 1990s have seen many of the NFL's great championship teams of the past return to the top.

The decade began with the New York Giants' victory in Super Bowl XXV. With two titles in five years, the Giants, one of the league's oldest franchises, returned to the top. Their Super Bowl XXV victory was assured when the Buffalo Bills missed a field goal that would have won the game. It was the first of four consecutive Super Bowl losses for the Bills, who were former AFL champions.

The rest of the early part of the decade was dominated by the Dallas Cowboys. The club had won Super Bowls VI and XII and appeared in Super Bowls V, X, and XIII in the 1970s. But they had suffered through some down years in the 1980s. By the early

CONTINUED ON PAGE 27

FOOTBALL FANS

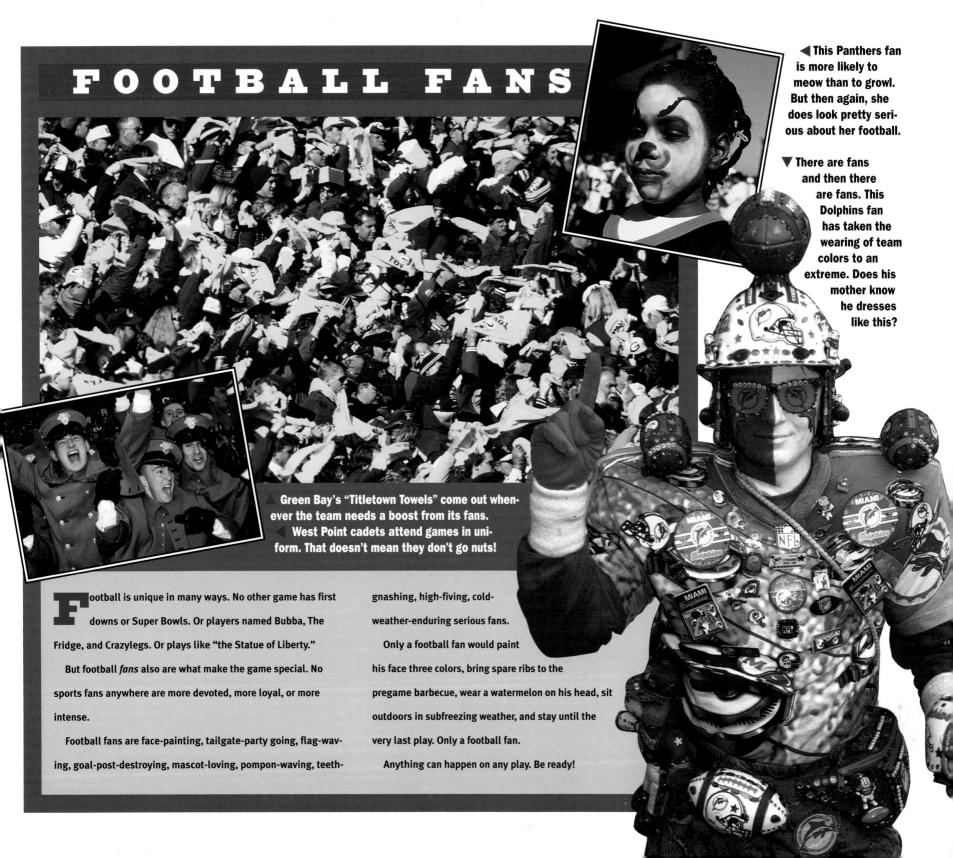

◀ This Panthers fan is more likely to meow than to growl. But then again, she does look pretty serious about her football.

▼ There are fans and then there are fans. This Dolphins fan has taken the wearing of team colors to an extreme. Does his mother know he dresses like this?

Green Bay's "Titletown Towels" come out whenever the team needs a boost from its fans.
◀ West Point cadets attend games in uniform. That doesn't mean they don't go nuts!

Football is unique in many ways. No other game has first downs or Super Bowls. Or players named Bubba, The Fridge, and Crazylegs. Or plays like "the Statue of Liberty."

But football *fans* also are what make the game special. No sports fans anywhere are more devoted, more loyal, or more intense.

Football fans are face-painting, tailgate-party going, flag-waving, goal-post-destroying, mascot-loving, pompon-waving, teeth-gnashing, high-fiving, cold-weather-enduring serious fans.

Only a football fan would paint his face three colors, bring spare ribs to the pregame barbecue, wear a watermelon on his head, sit outdoors in subfreezing weather, and stay until the very last play. Only a football fan.

Anything can happen on any play. Be ready!

The NFL's Most Successful Teams

Green Bay Packers
12 Championships

Chicago Bears
9 Championships

New York Giants
6 Championships

San Francisco 49ers
5 Championships

Dallas Cowboys
5 Championships

REDSKINS

Washington Redskins
5 Championships

NFL CHAMPIONS

From 1920-1932, the NFL champion was the team with the best regular-season record. From 1933-1969, the champion was the winner of the NFL Championship Game. Beginning with the 1970 season, the Super Bowl winner was champion of the NFL.

1997	Denver Broncos	1968	Baltimore Colts (NFL)	1947	Chicago Cardinals
1996	Green Bay Packers		New York Jets (AFL)	1946	Chicago Bears
1995	Dallas Cowboys	1967	Green Bay Packers (NFL)	1945	Cleveland Rams
1994	San Francisco 49ers		Oakland Raiders (AFL)	1944	Green Bay Packers
1993	Dallas Cowboys	1966	Green Bay Packers (NFL)	1943	Chicago Bears
1992	Dallas Cowboys		Kansas City Chiefs (AFL)	1942	Washington Redskins
1991	Washington Redskins	1965	Green Bay Packers (NFL)	1941	Chicago Bears
1990	New York Giants		Buffalo Bills (AFL)	1940*	Chicago Bears
1989	San Francisco 49ers	1964	Cleveland Browns (NFL)	1939	Green Bay Packers
1988	San Francisco 49ers		Buffalo Bills (AFL)	1938	New York Giants
1987	Washington Redskins	1963	Chicago Bears (NFL)	1937	Washington Redskins
1986	New York Giants		San Diego Chargers (AFL)	1936	Green Bay Packers
1985*	Chicago Bears	1962	Green Bay Packers (NFL)	1935	Detroit Lions
1984	San Francisco 49ers		Dallas Texans (AFL)	1934*	New York Giants
1983	Los Angeles Raiders	1961	Green Bay Packers (NFL)	1933	Chicago Bears
1982	Washington Redskins		Houston Oilers (AFL)	1932	Chicago Bears
1981	San Francisco 49ers	1960	Philadelphia Eagles (NFL)	1931	Green Bay Packers
1980	Oakland Raiders		Houston Oilers (AFL)	1930	Green Bay Packers
1979	Pittsburgh Steelers	1959	Baltimore Colts	1929	Green Bay Packers
1978	Pittsburgh Steelers	1958*	Baltimore Colts	1928	Providence Steam Roller
1977	Dallas Cowboys	1957	Detroit Lions	1927	New York Giants
1976	Oakland Raiders	1956	New York Giants	1926	Frankford Yellow Jackets
1975	Pittsburgh Steelers	1955	Cleveland Browns	1925	Chicago Cardinals
1974	Pittsburgh Steelers	1954	Cleveland Browns	1924	Cleveland Bulldogs
1973	Miami Dolphins	1953	Detroit Lions	1923	Canton Bulldogs
1972*	Miami Dolphins	1952	Detroit Lions	1922	Canton Bulldogs
1971	Dallas Cowboys	1951	Los Angeles Rams	1921	Chicago Staleys
1970	Baltimore Colts	1950*	Cleveland Browns	1920	Akron Pros
1969	Minnesota Vikings (NFL)	1949	Philadelphia Eagles		
	Kansas City Chiefs (AFL)	1948	Philadelphia Eagles		

*1934: The Giants won after changing into sneakers at halftime in order to get better traction on an icy field.

*1940: The Bears beat the Redskins 73-0, the most points ever scored by one team in an NFL game.

*1950: After joining the NFL from the AAFC, the Browns appeared in a record six consecutive NFL Championship Games.

*1958: Some call the overtime thriller in which the Colts defeated the Giants "The Greatest Game Ever Played."

*1972: The Dolphins' championship capped off the only undefeated, untied season in NFL history. Miami had a 17-0 record.

*1985: The Bears' huge defensive tackle William (Refrigerator) Perry ran for a touchdown on offense in Super Bowl XX.

CONTINUED FROM PAGE 24

1990s, they were back, led by top players such as quarterback Troy Aikman, running back Emmitt Smith, and wide receiver Michael Irvin. Dallas won three Super Bowls in four seasons (1992–95).

The first of those championships came on a mighty offensive display in a 52–17 defeat of Buffalo in Super Bowl XXVII. Dallas won the rematch in Super Bowl XVIII as well. The Cowboys defeated Pittsburgh in Super Bowl XXX, a rematch of Super Bowls X and XIII.

In 1996, another team with a great past added to its legend. The Green Bay Packers, who won the first two Super Bowls, won the big game again. Their 35–21 victory over New England brought the NFL's Super Bowl years full circle.

▲ Young stars like Arizona Cardinals defensive end Simeon Rice point the way to the NFL's future.

The NFL Today

The NFL today is made up of 30 teams playing in stadiums from Miami to Seattle and San Diego to New England. In the NFL's early days, most teams played in the Midwest and Northeast. Today, cities from coast to coast enjoy the fun and excitement of NFL games. The newest NFL teams are the Carolina Panthers and Jacksonville Jaguars, who joined the league in 1995. The Cleveland Browns will begin play again in 1999.

What is next for the NFL? Now that the league has conquered America, it is looking to spread the game to the rest of the world. Each summer in Europe, the NFL sponsors the six-team World League (below), which is bringing hard-hitting football action to new fans.

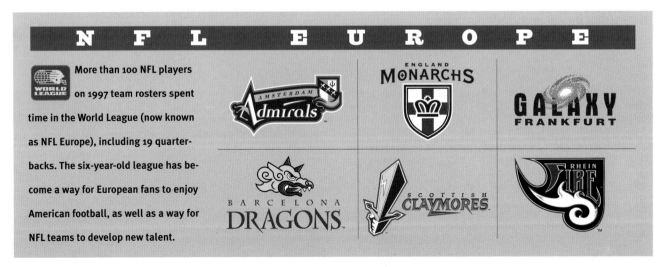

N F L   E U R O P E

More than 100 NFL players on 1997 team rosters spent time in the World League (now known as NFL Europe), including 19 quarterbacks. The six-year-old league has become a way for European fans to enjoy American football, as well as a way for NFL teams to develop new talent.

AMSTERDAM Admirals

ENGLAND MONARCHS

GALAXY FRANKFURT

BARCELONA DRAGONS

SCOTTISH CLAYMORES

RHEIN FIRE

Football Around the World

Football has been America's greatest game for more than 100 years. But did you know football has been played in Japan since the 1930s? And in Great Britain since the 1940s?

Football isn't as popular around the world as it is in America, but the game is growing internationally. There are amateur leagues in Australia, England, Germany, Italy, Japan, and Mexico.

One of the key ways that international fans follow the NFL is on television. People in more than 180 countries watch NFL games, many in their native languages. Who knows? Super Bowl LVII might be between London and Tokyo!

The sport of football is played in countries all over the world.

Today's NFL by the Numbers

2

Number of conferences in the NFL

6

Number of NFL divisions (3 per conference)

7

Number of on-field officials

12

Number of NFL teams that make the playoffs

12

Number of different teams that have won a Super Bowl

16

Number of games in a team's season

30

Number of NFL teams

A AMERICAN FOOTBALL CONFERENCE

EASTERN DIVISION

BUFFALO BILLS

INDIANAPOLIS COLTS

MIAMI DOLPHINS

NEW ENGLAND PATRIOTS

NEW YORK JETS

CENTRAL DIVISION

BALTIMORE RAVENS

CINCINNATI BENGALS

JACKSONVILLE JAGUARS

PITTSBURGH STEELERS

TENNESSEE OILERS

WESTERN DIVISION

DENVER BRONCOS

KANSAS CITY CHIEFS

OAKLAND RAIDERS

SAN DIEGO CHARGERS

SEATTLE SEAHAWKS

NATIONAL FOOTBALL CONFERENCE

EASTERN DIVISION

ARIZONA
CARDINALS

DALLAS
COWBOYS

NEW YORK
GIANTS

PHILADELPHIA
EAGLES

WASHINGTON
REDSKINS

CENTRAL DIVISION

CHICAGO
BEARS

DETROIT
LIONS

GREEN BAY
PACKERS

MINNESOTA
VIKINGS

TAMPA BAY
BUCCANEERS

WESTERN DIVISION

ATLANTA
FALCONS

CAROLINA
PANTHERS

NEW ORLEANS
SAINTS

ST. LOUIS
RAMS

SAN FRANCISCO
49ERS

Cleveland Browns franchise will begin play in 1999.

53
Number of players
on an NFL roster

79
Number of seasons
the NFL has played
(through 1998)

100
Number of yards in
an NFL field (not
including end zones)

194
Number of men
enshrined in the
Pro Football Hall
of Fame

305
Weight in pounds
of average Jaguars
lineman in 1997

3,600
Number of seconds
in an NFL game

133,000,000
Record number of
Americans who
watched Super Bowl
XXXII

WEATHER OR NOT

Nothing stops an NFL game. Not snow, not rain, not fog, mud, blizzard, or a plague of locusts. In the 1948 NFL Championship Game, the Eagles left the comfort of their parkas long enough to defeat the Cardinals 7–0.

The famous "Fog Bowl" was a 1988 NFC playoff game.
The Chicago Bears hosted the Philadelphia Eagles.
Everything was fine until a thick fog blanketed
Soldier Field late in the first half. The pea-soup-like
conditions made it tough for the fans to see, but the
players had few problems, and Chicago won 20–12.

WEATHER OR NOT

These Pennsylvania high school teams don't let a little mud get in the way of their game. The MVP is the guy who does the team laundry.

Flag football in Buffalo: "Cut left at the snowman and buttonhook on that icy patch. On three. Break!"

▲ This California peewee player doesn't care that he is wearing the ground. He came up with the ball.
▼ Now that's a happy Packer. Aaron Taylor is all smiles—and all mud—after a key win over the 49ers in Green Bay.

Joe Montana

Few players in any sport ever captured the world's attention as much as Joe Montana did. His great running, passing, and leadership propelled San Francisco to four Super Bowl triumphs. He was the MVP of Super Bowls XVI, XIX, and XXIV. Montana was a master of the last-minute comeback, as he proved in Super Bowl XXIII by firing the winning touchdown pass with only 34 seconds to play. Montana played 16 seasons (1979–1994), spending the last two years with Kansas City.

CHAPTER FOUR
NFL Supermen
The Dream Came True for a Special Few

The kid who tosses a football on a beach or in a park, the student who puts on a high school uniform, the young player who tries out for the college team...they all have the same dream: to play in the NFL.

Making that dream come true takes years of hard work, endless days of practice and workouts, and countless hours of running, stretching, and lifting.

From those players come a special few who rise above the rest. These are the superstars, the players even other players love to watch. They are masters of their craft.

The question is: Was all the hard work worth the result?

The only ones who can say for sure are the men on these pages. They have seen their dreams come true. They can look back to a peewee field in Mississippi, to a high school in Oklahoma, to a university in Florida, or even to an island in the South Pacific. They look back and remember what they went through to reach the top.

Most of these players, as great as they are, still are reaching. They return each season more determined than ever to succeed. And each year, new players come along, eager to knock the superstars off their perches. On the following pages, meet the players whose NFL dreams have come true.

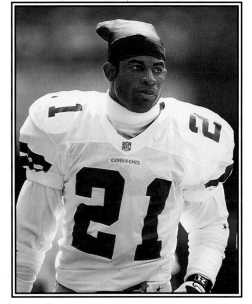

▲ **Deion Sanders**
The man known as Prime Time is one of the best two-sport players ever. An outstanding cornerback and wide reciever with Dallas, he also stars in baseball.

▲ **Walter Payton**
The man known as "Sweetness" for his slick running style retired after the 1987 season as the NFL's all-time leading rusher with 16,726 yards in 13 seasons with the Bears. In 1977, Payton set a single-game rushing record with 275 yards; in 1985, he helped Chicago win Super Bowl XX.

Packers Power

▲ Reggie White

Reggie White is the NFL's all-time leader in sacks. His powerful pass-rushing skills have led him to a record 12 Pro Bowls and helped Green Bay win Super Bowl XXXI. In that game, he set a record with 3 sacks. White, an ordained minister, also is a leader in the community, both in Green Bay and in his home state of Tennessee.

▶ Brett Favre

What hasn't Brett Favre done as quarterback of the Green Bay Packers? After the 1996 season, he led them to victory in Super Bowl XXXI. He is Green Bay's all-time leader in touchdown passes. In 1995 and 1996, Favre was the consensus choice as the NFL's most valuable player. The strong-armed young man from tiny Kiln, Mississippi, is one of the NFL's top players.

Dallas Dynamite

▲ **Emmitt Smith**

In 1995, Emmitt Smith set an NFL record with 25 touchdowns, helping the Dallas Cowboys win their third Super Bowl in four seasons. Speedy and durable, Smith was a key part of those championship teams. He was the MVP of Super Bowl XXVIII. Smith, a former University of Florida All-America, ranks second on the NFL's all-time list for rushing touchdowns.

◄ **Troy Aikman**

Few quarterbacks in history can boast the postseason success of Troy Aikman. From 1992–95, he led the Cowboys to four NFC Championship Games and three Super Bowl victories. He was the MVP of Super Bowl XXVII, and holds the all-time postseason record for completion percentage. When the game is big, Aikman seems to play bigger. Aikman grew up in California and Oklahoma, and was a top college quarterback at UCLA.

Fabulous 49ers

▲ Steve Young
From 1991–97, Steve Young had the NFL's highest passer rating in six of seven seasons, including an all-time record 112.8 in 1994. After that season, he led the 49ers to a victory in Super Bowl XXIX. With a record 6 touchdown passes, Steve was named the game's MVP. The left-handed passer has been named to six Pro Bowls. At Brigham Young University, Young set numerous NCAA passing records.

▶ Jerry Rice
There have been so many great players in NFL history, it is hard to say one is best. But Jerry Rice *is* the best wide receiver in NFL history. In 13 seasons with San Francisco, he has become the NFL's all-time leader in touchdowns, receptions, and receiving yardage. Rice, a product of Mississippi Valley State, combines outstanding hands with great speed and an uncanny ability to get open in the clutch.

Passing Fancy

▲ John Elway

If the Denver Broncos are trailing with little time left...never fear, the Comeback King is here! In 15 seasons with Denver, Elway has led his team from behind in the fourth quarter 41 times. He also has led them to three AFC Championships, and has been named to eight Pro Bowls. Elway was an All-America quarterback at Stanford.

◄ Dan Marino

Talk about NFL passing records begins and ends with Miami's Dan Marino. In 15 seasons, he has become the NFL's all-time leader in attempts, completions, passing yardage, and touchdown passes. He is known for his ability to lead comebacks, and for his super-quick release of the football. A native of Pittsburgh, Marino set career passing records at his hometown University of Pittsburgh.

Dominant Defenders

▲ Junior Seau

Junior's last name is pronounced "SAY-ow." And that's just what ball carriers do when he tackles them. In eight seasons with the San Diego Chargers, Seau has been named to seven Pro Bowl teams. One of football's toughest players, he plays the pass as well as he plays the run. He helped San Diego reach Super Bowl XXIX. Junior, whose real name is Tiaina, was born in San Diego but raised on the island of Samoa.

▶ Bruce Smith

This pass-rushing machine twice has been named the NFL defensive player of the year (1990 and 1996). He is second all-time in sacks, and holds the NFL career postseason record for most sacks. In 13 years with Buffalo, Smith has played on four AFC championship teams. A Virginia native, he was an All-America player at Virginia Tech.

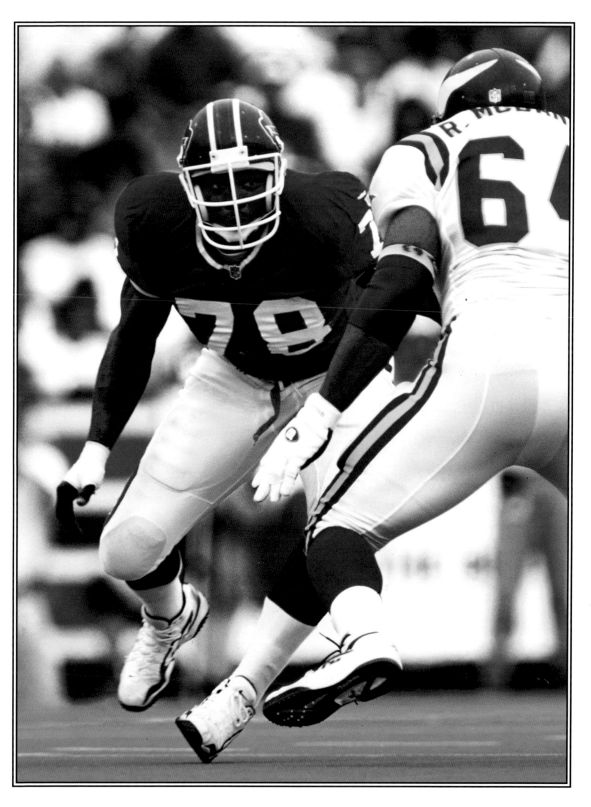

Awesome Offense

▲ Barry Sanders
This Detroit Lions runner has more moves than a belly dancer. Since 1989, Sanders has dazzled fans and tacklers alike with his changes of direction, his bursts through the hole, and his 360-degree spins. He has rushed for more than 1,000 yards in a record nine consecutive seasons, has won four NFL rushing titles, and ranks second all time in the NFL in rushing, after gaining 2,053 yards in 1997. At Oklahoma State, he won the Heisman Trophy as a junior.

◄ Drew Bledsoe
In only five seasons, Bledsoe has become one of the top quarterbacks in the NFL. He led New England to Super Bowl XXXI. In 1994, he set an NFL single-season record with 691 pass attempts. That season, Bledsoe also set records for most attempts (70) and most completions (45) in one game. Bledsoe was the NFL's number-one draft choice in 1993 out of Washington State.

WOW! HOW DID THEY DO THAT?

San Diego's Gary Anderson gets some serious
flying time before crash-landing in the end zone
for a touchdown.

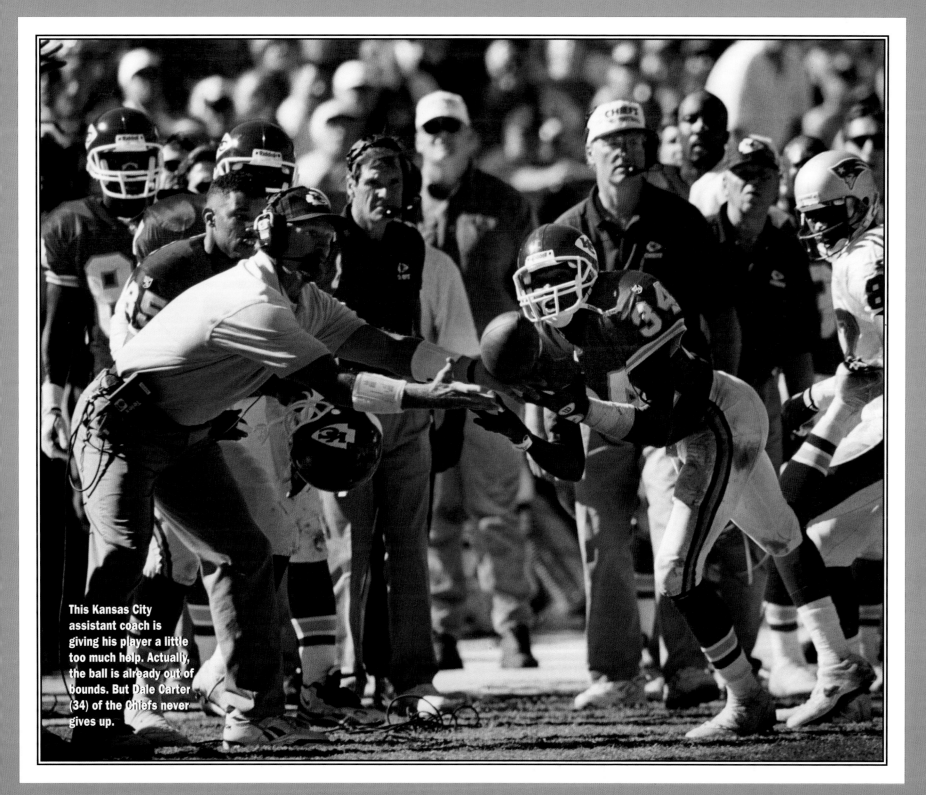

This Kansas City assistant coach is giving his player a little too much help. Actually, the ball is already out of bounds. But Dale Carter (34) of the Chiefs never gives up.

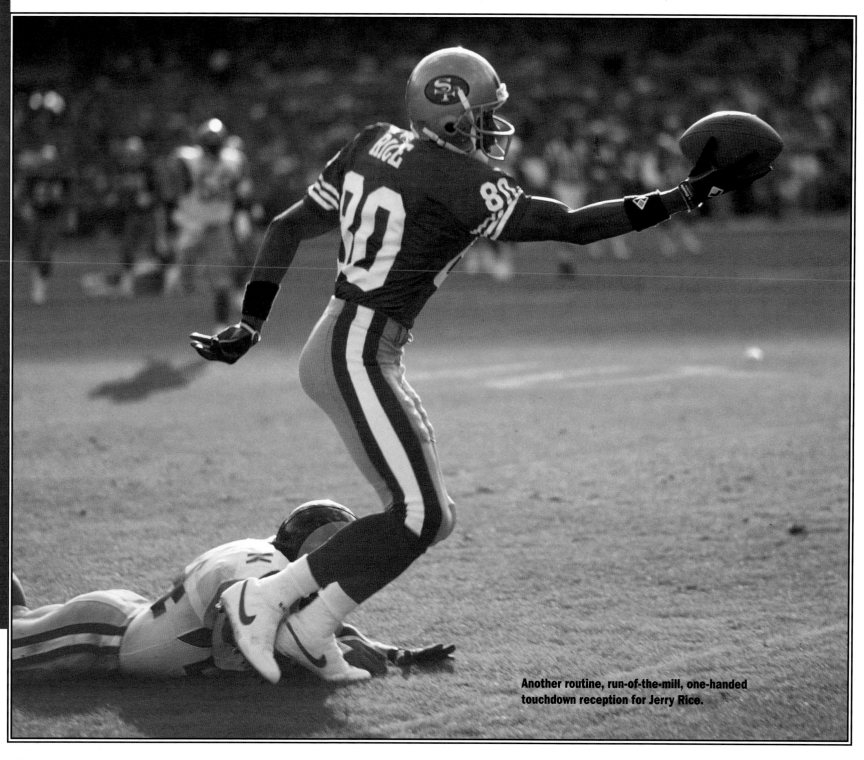

Another routine, run-of-the-mill, one-handed touchdown reception for Jerry Rice.

Flags (and bodies) are flying as the Jets and Dolphins tangle.
This photo won the Hall of Fame photography contest for best
NFL action picture of 1997.

45

WOW! HOW DID THEY DO THAT?

Despite Darrien Gordon's best efforts, Cincinnati's Carl Pickens made this fingertip catch. The Denver assistant coach in the background just can't believe his eyes.

Two men went up for the ball...and one came down with it.
Dallas's Michael Irvin wrestled this touchdown catch away from
Pittsburgh's Chad Scott.

CHAPTER FIVE

Game Day USA

Football Is a Coast-to-Coast Tradition

▲ The tundra may be frozen, but the sausages are well done outside legendary Lambeau Field on game day. Many fans agree that pregame tailgate parties are half the fun of attending the big game.

Football is celebrated from Alaska to Florida, from Maine to Hawaii, and everywhere in between. People flock to games throughout the fall.

One of the great things about football is tradition. Ever since the game came to college campuses and NFL stadiums, tradition has been as much a part of football as goal posts.

What makes a tradition? Time, more than anything else. Fans today take part in the same traditions as their parents and grandparents. The tradition of football is what joins generations together.

Traditions can be as simple as a bonfire the night before a game or a particular cheer that students have used for many years.

At Washington Redskins games, fans join in

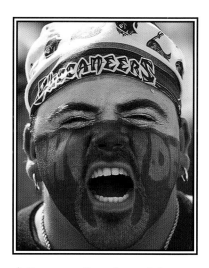

▲ The pregame introduction of the players, such as the 49ers' Garrison Hearst (above), excites football fans.

singing "Hail to the Redskins," the most famous fight song in the NFL. Before the Army-Navy game in Philadelphia, the cadets of both schools march onto the field and then into the stands.

At the University of California, no student wears red clothing to games because that is the color of their archrival, Stanford.

At high schools rooting for everything from six-man teams in Texas to national powers in Ohio and Florida, teams burst through banners held by the pep squad.

Families have traditions, too. At the home stadiums of long-time NFL teams such as the Giants, Packers, or Bears, three generations of fans from one family crowd around the pregame barbecue.

Tradition will be around as long as there are football fans—and football games.

▲ Fans as well as players bring their "game faces" to the stadium. The players are limited to eyeblack, but fans such as this artistic Tampa Bay supporter can go all out.

◀ University of Colorado fans go as wild as their mascot, a buffalo named Ralphie, leads the football team onto the field.

"What happens is you realize you're part of something that's a whole lot bigger than yourself. You walk onto that field, look around and you say 'I can't let these people down.'"

— **Britt Hager**
former Permian High School
All-America and NFL player

When it is time for the big game, everything stops. Everyone in town turns out to watch. And the players take part in something they will remember for the rest of their lives.

The Big Game

Rivalries between teams that have played each other for decades are one of football's best traditions.

The high school games between Masillon and McKinley in Ohio, Odessa and Permian in Texas, and Garfield and Roosevelt in Los Angeles are three examples of rivalries that involve generations of people in a single town.

In college, students and alumni look forward each year to the game against their traditional foe. Among the most famous of these rivalries are Michigan versus Ohio State, Harvard versus Yale, Florida versus Florida State, Oklahoma versus Texas, USC versus UCLA, and Auburn versus Alabama. One small-school rivalry, Lehigh versus Lafayette, is more than 100 years old.

NFL teams have rivalries as well. Some are regional, some date back to the NFL's earliest days. Whenever Washington and Dallas play, pay no attention to the won-lost records because the game is going to be a war. The same is true of Kansas City and Oakland, Detroit and Chicago, and Green Bay and Minnesota.

▲ A hopeful Green Bay Packers fan.
▼ It's just not an NFL game unless you see a shouting bunch of face-painted guys wearing funny hats.

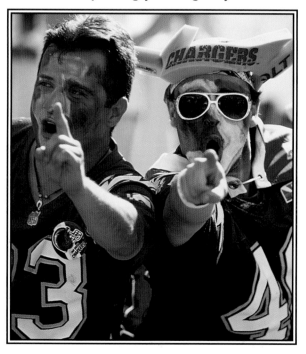

▲ Hey, this is the Navy, not the Air Force! Young sailors go flying as they cheer for their school.

▲ This Chiefs fan is ready to take on the weather.
▼ A pregame flyover by jets is an ear-blasting thrill.

▲ The Michigan Wolverines take the field! When a team charges out of the tunnel, it charges up the fans.

THE BIG GAME

▲ Like father, like Thomas, like son. Honoring Derrick Thomas, their favorite Kansas City Chiefs player, this father-and-son team head for their seats.

▶ Gimme a B, gimme an A, gimme a D, gimme a G... Eventually, these University of Wisconsin cheerleaders will lead the crowd in spelling "Badgers."

▲ At halftime, the players have plenty to do: get some water, retape their ankles, listen to their coaches' instructions. But the fans in the stands enjoy entertainment that ranges from marching bands to Frisbee-catching dogs.

◄ Another way to fire up the crowd is with a costumed mascot. This fiery warrior leads the San Diego State Aztecs out onto the field. Good thing it's usually warm in San Diego.

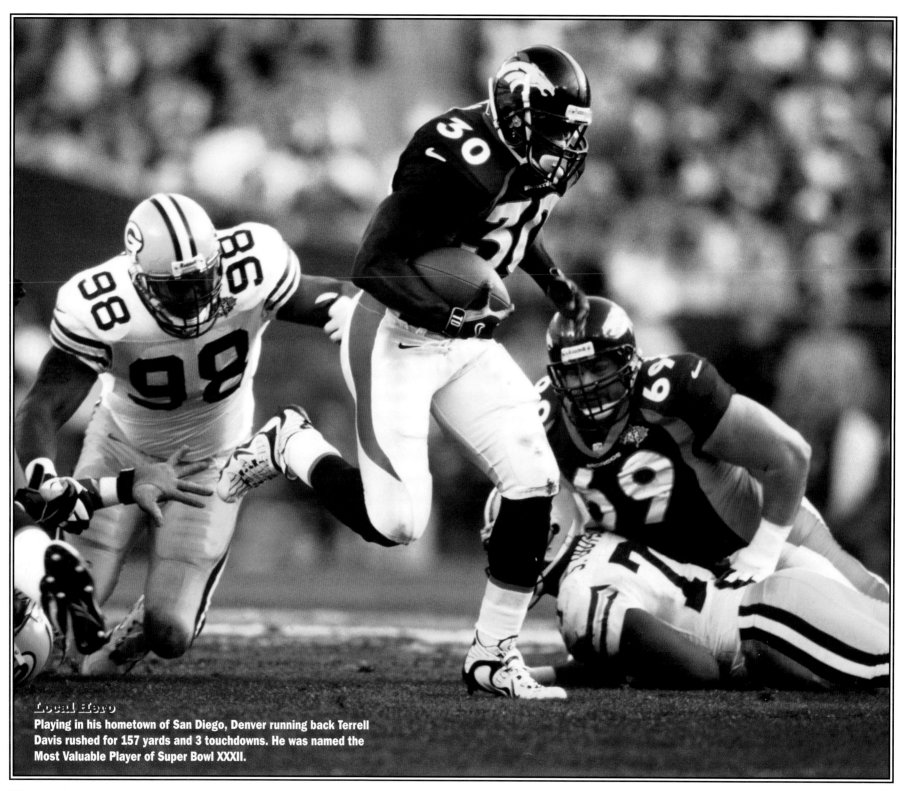

Local Hero
Playing in his hometown of San Diego, Denver running back Terrell Davis rushed for 157 yards and 3 touchdowns. He was named the Most Valuable Player of Super Bowl XXXII.

CHAPTER SIX

Super Bowl XXXII

Was It the Best Ever?

A few days before Super Bowl XXXII, Denver running back Terrell Davis went to school. Or rather, *back* to school. In 1991, Davis graduated from Lincoln High School in southeast San Diego. Now he was back in his hometown to play in Super Bowl XXXII. Lincoln held a special assembly at which it retired his high school uniform number (which was 7).

Davis spoke to the students before he returned to practice for the big game.

"Don't let anyone steal your dreams," he told them. "You can do anything you set your mind to. Never, never give up."

On January 25, 1998, Davis and the Broncos didn't let anyone steal their dreams of a Super Bowl championship. Denver defeated the defending-champion Green Bay Packers 31-24 in what may have been the best Super Bowl ever played.

The victory capped a dream season for Davis. He led the AFC with 1,750 yards rushing and was named to his second Pro Bowl.

The game also topped off a dream career for quarterback John Elway. The 15-year veteran is second all-time in passing yards and is an eight-time Pro Bowl selection. Elway also had led the Broncos to the Super Bowl three times before. On his fourth try, he finally won.

Davis was the hometown hero, though. He ran for 157 yards and a Super Bowl-record 3 touchdowns. He was awarded the Pete Rozelle Trophy as the Super Bowl's Most Valuable Player.

"I'm just kind of numb," Davis said. "To come back here to where I grew up and win this award, wow! This is really special."

SUPER BOWL XXXII

Denver Broncos 31

Green Bay Packers 24

SUPER XXXII BOWL

▲ Green Bay's Brett Favre threw 3 touchdown passes, but they weren't enough to overcome Denver.

The Broncos' victory was even more special because it was the first by an AFC team since the Raiders won Super Bowl XVIII. The NFC had won the previous 13 Super Bowls.

Most experts expected Green Bay to extend the streak to 14. Packers quarterback Brett Favre had been the NFL's MVP for three years in a row (he shared the honor in 1997 with Detroit's Barry Sanders). Green Bay also had dominated the 49ers and the NFL's number-one defense in the NFC Championship Game.

Denver was a wild-card entry into the AFC playoffs, and had to win three playoff games to earn a trip to San Diego. A wild-card team had won the Super Bowl only once before (the Raiders won Super Bowl XV). Only loyal Denver fans and the Broncos themselves thought Denver had a chance.

The Packers scored on the first possession of the game on a touchdown pass from Favre to wide receiver Antonio Freeman. But the Broncos evened the score on the next series when Davis ran for a 1-yard touchdown. After safety Tyrone Braxton intercepted a pass by Favre, Elway led the Broncos to their second touchdown. He scored on a 1-yard run, becoming, at age

▲ Mark Chmura made a great touchdown reception of a pass by Brett Favre, as Tyrone Braxton came up inches short.

37, the oldest player to score in a Super Bowl.

Denver kicker Jason Elam made the score 17-7 with a 51-yard field goal, the second-longest in Super Bowl history. But Favre led the Packers on a 95-yard drive that ended with a sensational touchdown catch by tight end Mark Chmura in the final seconds of the first half.

▲ Every Broncos fan was returning this Mile High Salute from Terrell Davis after he won the Super Bowl MVP award.

Although Davis was a hero most of the day, he fumbled on Denver's first play of the second half. Green Bay tied the score on a 27-yard field goal by Ryan Longwell.

Another long drive by the Broncos ended with Davis's second touchdown. Soon after the fourth quarter started, Favre and Freeman hooked up again for a touchdown pass that tied the score at 24-24, the third tie of the game.

After both defenses held twice, the Broncos got the ball at Green Bay's 49-yard line with 3 minutes 27 seconds left in the game. If they could score, then hold Green Bay, the game would be over.

That's just what Denver did.

Elway used all his offensive weapons to move the ball downfield. Davis's 17-yard run took the Broncos to the 1-yard line. On the next play, with 1 minute 47 seconds remaining, Davis strolled through a huge hole in the line to score the winning touchdown.

The Broncos were the new NFL champions. It was a dream come true.

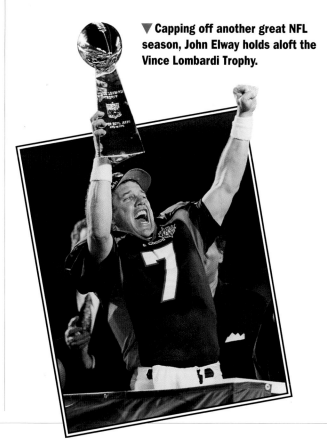

▼ Capping off another great NFL season, John Elway holds aloft the Vince Lombardi Trophy.

FUTURE SUPER BOWLS

XXXIII
January 31, 1999
MIAMI, FLORIDA

XXXIV
January 30, 2000
ATLANTA, GEORGIA

XXXV
January 28, 2001
TAMPA, FLORIDA

SUPER BOWL XXXII

Shannon was Sharpe. The Denver tight end, here trying to avoid Packers linebacker Bernardo Harris, led the Broncos with 5 catches and made key blocks to help Terrell Davis.

SUPER BOWL XXXII

A herd of Broncos converges on Green Bay running back Dorsey Levens.

DENVER BRONCOS VS. GREEN BAY PACKERS

After Denver linebacker John Mobley knocked down this final Green Bay pass intended for Mark Chmura, the Broncos were one kneel-down play away from their first Super Bowl championship.

▲ A big hit forces a fumble by Antonio Freeman.
▼ Photographers focused on a great football game.

▲ Oh, yes! Denver defensive end Neil Smith's face says it all, as tears of joy mix with Super Bowl sweat.

Read more about football, the NFL, and the NFL kids' programs mentioned below when you visit the official NFL kids' web site. Click Play Football! at http://www.nfl.com

MAKE THE PERFECT PASS

Dan Marino (see page 39) offers these tips for making a great pass:

1 With your hand toward one end of the ball, get a good grip on the laces.

2 Hold the ball near your ear, and turn your shoulder toward your target. Step forward with your front foot as you throw.

3 Follow through with your throwing arm across your body. For a good spiral, the ball should roll off the ends of your fingers.

Get Into the Game!

DON'T STAY ON THE SIDELINES...PLAY FOOTBALL

After reading about the excitement of Super Bowl XXXII, the question is: What Super Bowl will you play in? Every player in Super Bowl XXXII started out like you, a young football fan and player. The players practiced hard, and their Super Bowl dreams came true. Here are a few ways you can help make your Super Bowl dreams come true:

Flag football: Many local recreation departments sponsor flag football leagues for boys and girls. Instead of a play ending when a ball carrier is tackled, it ends when a defender pulls a flag off the ball carrier's belt. Flag football is fun and safe. The NFL sponsors NFL Flag leagues in many cities; players wear jerseys with real NFL logos. (Call 800-NFL-SNAP for more information.)

Tackle football: When players are old enough, they can begin playing tackle football in youth leagues. Pop Warner is the largest youth football organization, but there are many national and local leagues. Players wear helmets and pads just like the pros. (Contact your local youth football league for more details.)

Skills competitions: Each year, more than 600,000 boys and girls take part in the NFL/Gatorade Punt, Pass & Kick contest. Ask your local recreation department about the date and location of the PP&K event near you. (Call 800-NFL-SNAP for the competition near you.)

Just playing around: While organized leagues are fun, you don't need an official team to play football. Try Dan Marino's passing tips (see box) next time you are playing with your friends.

Have fun, keep playing America's greatest game, and who knows? Maybe someday you'll hold the Vince Lombardi Trophy over your head after winning the Super Bowl!